Contents

Published by Pedigree Books Limited
Beech Hill House, Walnut Gardens, Exeter, Devon EX4 4DG.
E-mail books@pedigreegroup.co.uk
Published 2003

Licensing by:

Hasbro

Consumer
Products

£6.99

Meet the Ponies

Sunny Daze

The very first time you meet Sunny Daze, watch out! She's so friendly, she'll nearly bowl you over running right up to you and giggling, "Hi! Want to play?"

Rainbow Dash

Rainbow Dash is the most outrageous Pony you'll ever meet! When it comes to adventure, excitement and fun, if Rainbow Dash hasn't done it, it's never been done!

Pinkie Pie

Pinkie Pie is the sweetest lamb of a Pony who loves trying new, fun things, but sometimes she gets just a little bit nervous.

Sparkleworks

Have you ever flown over Ponyland in a hot air balloon? You haven't? Then you need to go for a ride with Sparkleworks.

Kimono

Kimono is the most wise and knowing Pony in all of Ponyland. Kimono tells of times past, like when the forests were filled with beautiful Unicorns.

Minty

Did you know that Minty collects socks? No one in Ponyland even wears socks let alone collects them! No one, that is, except Minty.

Wysteria

Wysteria is the best listener in all of Ponyland. She is gentle and kind and loves to surprise her friends!

Sweetberry

Sweetberry can whip up a Cocoa Mocha Rainbowberry Peanut Butter Float or a Key Lime Blueberry Liquorice Graham Cracker Pie like no one else can! You're going to have a blast with Sweetberry.

my little Pony

Rainbow Dash

A Pony's Tale

by Jodi Huelin

illustrated by Ken Edwards

The ponies gathered at the Castle.
Excitement was in the air.
It was the day to begin this year's Pony Play!

"I hope I get a part in the play," said Minty.
"Me, too," said Pinkie Pie.
All of the waiting was making her nervous.

"I want to play someone important," said Rainbow Dash.
Wysteria didn't want to be *in* the show.
She preferred a role behind the scenes.

Soon, all of the ponies' wishes came true.
"Look!" squealed Minty. "I get to play a clown!"
"I will play the princess!" exclaimed Rainbow Dash.

Congratulations
to the
following ponies:
Minty .... Clown

"I get to be a ballerina!" said Pinkie Pie.
Wysteria was excited.
She would design all of the sets for the play.
Painting was her specialty.

Rainbow Dash..... Princess

Pinkie Pie....... Ballerin*

The Crew

Cotton Candy..... Director*

Wysteria...... Set Desi*

Kimono........

Cotton Candy was chosen to be the director.
She was a natural storyteller.

The ponies got down to work.
They practiced every day, rain or shine.

Cotton Candy wanted the play to be perfect.
She took her job as director very seriously.
She followed the script exactly.

"Let's play a game in one of the scenes,"
suggested Sunny Daze.
"We can't," Cotton Candy said.
"That's not in the script."

"I think the princess should sit on a throne,"
said Rainbow Dash.
"No, that won't work," said Cotton Candy.
"The script says the princess should stand."

"I could tell a joke!" Minty suggested.
"Clowns are perfect joke-tellers."
Cotton Candy wasn't so sure.

Cotton Candy liked the sets, but she asked Wysteria,
"Can they be more like the ones described in the script?"

"I think Wysteria's set designs are beautiful!" said Minty.
"Me, too," added Rainbow Dash. "I wouldn't change
a thing."

"If we pay perfect attention to the script, our play will also be perfect!" Cotton Candy said. She didn't realize that the other ponies' suggestions might make the play even better.

With just a few days to go until the play,
Cotton Candy noticed something.

The ponies were still working hard on the play,
but they didn't seem excited about it anymore.

I should have listened to my friends, Cotton Candy realized. They all had great ideas. So what if we don't follow the script perfectly. If we add in everyone's ideas, the play will be better than perfect— it will be FUN!

So Cotton Candy called a meeting.

"I want to apologize," said Cotton Candy.
I didn't listen to your ideas because I was worried the play
wouldn't be perfect if we changed it," she said.

Cotton Candy promised that from now on,
the play would use *all* of the ponies' ideas.
The ponies were so happy.
"Hooray for Cotton Candy!" they cheered.

When the day of the play arrived, everyone was nervous.
But they needn't have worried.
Wysteria's sets were beautiful.
Princess Rainbow Dash sat on a sparkly throne.

Everyone laughed at Minty's joke,
and played along with the game that Sunny Daze invented.

"A Pony Tale" was a wonderful success.
"Thanks to wonderful friends!" said Cotton Candy.

Colouring Fun Pages

Sunny Daze loves to dance.

Sparkleworks invites her friends

Find Rainbow Dash at the costume party.

Pinkie Pie's Spooky Dream

by Jodi Huelin

illustrated by Ken Edwards

It was a perfect night in Ponyville.
The sky was clear. The air smelled sweet.
Millions of stars twinkled high above.

"Let's sleep outside tonight!" said Sparkleworks.
"That's a great idea," said Rainbow Dash.
"Count me in!" Pinkie Pie added.

So the ponies gathered their coziest blankets,
and headed out to find the perfect spot.

They settled down on a nice grassy meadow
with a view of the stars.

"Let's tell spooky stories!" suggested Rainbow Dash.
"S-s-spooky?" asked Pinkie Pie.

"One night, long, long ago, there was a pony with pretty,
pink hair," Rainbow Dash started.
"Like me?" asked Pinkie Pie.
"Exactly like you," said Rainbow Dash.

"The pony was on her way to the Castle,
but there was a terrible storm," Rainbow Dash continued.
"It was very dark, so she used the moon as a guide.
But then, big, thick clouds covered the moon.

The pony walked and walked,
but never found the Castle.
She was lost in the woods,
and no pony ever heard from her again."

"Never?" asked Pinkie Pie.
"Never ever," answered Rainbow Dash. "But sometimes the wind sounds like her voice calling, `Woo, wooooo.´"

"I hope that there isn't a storm tonight," Pinkie Pie said. Sparkleworks smiled. "Don't worry, Pinkie Pie," she said. "It's just an old pony story. I've heard it a million times."

It was late, so the ponies lay down to sleep.
Sparkleworks and Rainbow Dash drifted off right away.
But not Pinkie Pie.
She kept thinking about the story.

As she looked up at the stars,
Pinkie Pie thought about that pony with the pink hair.
Could she still be out there, lost?
Pinkie Pie wondered.

Eventually Pinkie Pie fell asleep,
but unlike Sparkleworks and Rainbow Dash,
Pinkie Pie did not sleep well.
She had a terrible dream.

In Pinkie Pie's dream,
the night was cloudy.
She was walking to the Castle
when rain started to pour from the sky.

Pinkie Pie used the moon to guide her—
until a cloud blocked the moon.
``I can't see anything!'' Pinkie Pie exclaimed.

She kept walking and walking,
but she couldn't find the Castle.
"I'm lost!" cried Pinkie Pie. "Lost! Lost! Lost!"

Pinkie Pie wasn't just talking in her dream.
She was calling out in her sleep,
and she woke her friends up.

"Pinkie Pie, wake up!" Sparkleworks said.
"You're having a bad dream," Rainbow Dash added.
Pinkie Pie woke up, startled.

"I was lost," Pinkie Pie said.
"Lost?" asked Rainbow Dash.
"No. You're on a sleepover under the stars
with Sparkleworks and me."

"I was trying to find the Castle, but it was dark,
and I kept walking . . ." said Pinkie Pie.
Then Sparkleworks and Rainbow Dash understood.
The story Rainbow Dash told had scared Pinkie Pie.
It caused her to have a bad dream.

"That was just a story," said Sparkleworks.
"It's not real."
"She's right," Rainbow Dash said.
"I heard it a long time ago at a sleepover party."

"Dreams can seem real," Sparkleworks said.
"But they're not."
"You're our friend. We'd never let you get lost,"
said Rainbow Dash.
"Friendship is real!" said Pinkie Pie.

After the ponies went back to sleep,
they had nothing but happy dreams.
The next morning, they went to the Café for breakfast.
"Happy dreams are nice," said Pinkie Pie.
"But nothing is better than REAL, good friends!"

Colouring Fun Page